Artaud the Mômo

Artaud the Mômo

Translated and with notes by
Clayton Eshleman

Edited and with an Afterword by
Stephen Barber

DIAPHANES

THE RETURN OF
ARTAUD, THE MÔMO

LE RETOUR

D'ARTAUD, LE MÔMO

L'esprit ancré,
vissé en moi
par la poussée
psycho-lubrique
du ciel
est celui qui pense
toute tentation,
tout désir,
toute inhibition.

o dédi
a dada orzoura
o dou zoura
a dada skizi

o kaya
o kaya pontoura
o ponoura
a pena
poni

THE RETURN
OF ARTAUD, THE MÔMO

The anchored spirit,
screwed into me
by the psycho-
lubricious thrust
of the sky
is the one who thinks
every temptation,
every desire,
every inhibition.

o dedi
o dada orzoura
o dou zoura
a dada skizi

o kaya
o kaya pontoura
o ponoura
a pena
poni

C'est la toile d'araignée pentrale,
la poile onoure
d'ou-ou la voile,
la plaque anale d'anavou.

(Tu ne lui enlèves rien, dieu,
parce que c'est moi.
Tu ne m'as jamais rien enlevé de cet ordre.
Je l'écris ici pour la première fois,
je le trouve pour la première fois.)

Non la membrane de la voûte,
non le membre omis de ce foutre,
d'une déprédation issu,

mais une carne,
hors membrane,
hors de là où c'est dur ou mou.

Ja passée par le dur et mou,
étendue cette carne en paume,
tirée, tendue comme une paume
                    de main
exsangue de se tenir raide,
noir, violette
de tendre au mou.

Mais quoi donc à la fin, toi, le fou ?

It's the penetral* spider veil,
the female onor fur
of either-or the sail,
the anal plate of anayor.

(You lift nothing from it, god,
because it's me.
You never lifted anything of this order from me.
I'm writing it here for the first time,
I'm finding it for the first time.)

Not the membrane of the chasm,
nor the member omitted from this jism,
issued from a depredation,

but an old bag,*
outside membrane,
outside of there where it's hard or soft.

B'now passed through the hard and soft,
spread out this old bag in palm,
pulled, stretched like a palm
                of hand
bloodless from keeping rigid,
black, violet
from stretching to soft.

But what then in the end, you, the madman?

Moi ?

Cette langue entre quatre gencives,

cette viande entre deux genoux,

ce morceau de trou
pour les fous.

Mais justement pas pour les fous.
Pour les honnêtes,
que rabote un délire à rôter partout,

et qui de ce rot
firent la feuille,

écoutez bien :
firent la feuille
du début des générations,
dans la carne palmée de mes trous,
à moi.

Lesquels, et de quoi ces trous ?

D'âme, d'esprit, de moi, et d'être;
mais à la place où l'on s'en fout,
père, mère, Artaud et itou.

Me?

This tongue between four gums,

this meat between two knees,

this piece of hole
for madmen.

Yet precisely not for madmen.
For respectable men,
whom a delirium to belch everywhere planes,

and who from this belch
made the leaf,

listen closely:
made the leaf
of the beginning of generations
in the palmate old bag of my holes,
mine.

Which holes, holes of what?

Of soul, of spirit, of me, and of being;
but in the place where no one gives a shit,
father, mother, Artaud and artoo.

Dans l'humus de la trame à roues,
dans l'humus soufflant de la trame
de ce vide,
entre dur et mou.

Noir et violet,
raide,
pleutre
et c'est tout.

Ce qui veut dire qu'il y a un os,
où

dieu
s'est mis sur le poète,
pour lui saccager l'ingestion
de ses vers,
tels des pêts de tête
qu'il lui soutire par le con,

qu'il lui soutirerait du fond des âges,
jusqu'au fond de son trou de con,

et ce n'est pas un tour de con
qu'il lui joue de cette manière,
c'est le tour de toute la terre
contre qui a des couilles
au con.

Et si on ne comprend pas l'image,
— et c'est ce que je vous entends dire

In the humus of the plot with wheels,
in the breathing humus of the plot
of this void,
between hard and soft.

Black, violet,
rigid,
recreant
and that's all.

Which means that there is a bone,
where

god
sat down on the poet,
in order to sack the ingestion
of his lines,
like the head farts
that he wheedles out of him through his cunt,

that he would wheedle out of him from the
                              bottom of the ages,
down to the bottom of his cunt hole,

and it's not a cunt prank
that he plays on him in this way,
it's the prank of the whole earth
against whoever has balls
in his cunt.

And if you don't get the image,
— and that's what I hear you saying

en rond,
que vous ne comprenez pas l'image
qui est au fond
de mon trou de con, —

c'est que vous ignorez le fond,
non pas des choses,
mais de mon con
à moi,
bien que depuis le fond des âges
vous y clapotiez tous en rond
comme on clabaude un aliénage,
complote à mort une incarcération.

ge re ghi
regheghi
geghena
a reghena
a gegha
riri

Entre le cu et la chemise,
entre le foutre et l'infra-mise,
entre le membre et le faux bond,
entre la membrane et la lame,
entre la latte et le plafond,
entre le sperme et l'explosion,
tre l'arête et tre le limon,

in a circle,
that you don't get the image
which is at the bottom
of my cunt hole, —

it's because you don't know the bottom,
not of things,
but of my cunt,
mine,
although since the bottom of the ages
you've all been lapping there in a circle
as if badmouthing an alienage,[*]
plotting an incarceration to death.

> **ge re ghi**
> **regheghi**
> **geghena**
> **a reghena**
> **a gegha**
> **riri**

Between the ass and the shirt,
between the gism and the under-bet,
between the member and the let down,
between the membrane and the blade,
between the slat and the ceiling,
between the sperm and the explosion,
'tween the fishbone and 'tween the slime,

entre le cu et la main mise
                    de tous
sur la trappe à haute pression
d'un râle d'éjaculation
n'est pas un point
ni une pierre

éclatée morte au pied d'un bond

ni le membre coupe d'une âme
(l'âme n'est plus qu'un vieux dicton)
mais l'atterrante suspension
d'un souffle d'aliénation

violé, tondu, pompé à fond
par toute l'insolente racaille
de tous les empafrés d'étrons
qui n'eurent pas d'autre boustifaille
                    pour vivre
                    que de bouffer
                    Artaud
                    mômo
                    là, où l'on peut piner plus tôt
                    que moi
                    et l'autre bander plus haut
                    que moi
                    en moi-même
s'il a eu soin de mettre la tête
sur la courbure de cet os

between the ass and everyone's
                    seizure
of the high-pressure trap
of an ejaculation death rattle
is neither a point
nor a stone

burst dead at the foot of a bound

nor the severed member of a soul
(the soul is no more than an old saw)
but the terrifying suspension
of a breath of alienation

raped, clipped, completely sucked off
by all the insolent riff-raff
of all the turd-buggered
who had no other grub
                    in order to live
                    than to gobble
                    Artaud
                    mômo
                    there, where one can fuck sooner
                    than me
                    and the other get hard higher
                    than me
                    in myself
if he has taken care to put his head
on the curvature of that bone

situé entre anus et sexe,

de cet os sarclé que je dis

dans la crasse
d'un paradis
dont le premier dupé sur terre
ne fut pas le père ou la mère
qui dans cet antre te refit
                    mais
                    JE
vissé dans ma folie.

Et qu'est-ce qui me prit
d'y rouler moi aussi ma vie ?
                    MOI,
                    RIEN, *rien*.
Parce que moi,
                    j'y suis,
                    j'y suis
et c'est la vie
qui y roule sa paume obscène.

          Bien.
          Et après ?

          Après ? Après ?
          Le vieil Artaud
          est enterré

located between anus and sex,

              of that hoed bone that I say

in the filth
of a paradise
whose first dupe on earth
was not father nor mother
who diddled you in this den
              but
              I
screwed into my madness.

And what seized hold of me
that I too rolled my life there?
              ME,
              NOTHING, *nothing*.
Because I,
              I am there,
              I'm there
and it is life
that rolls its obscene palm there.

              Ok.
              And afterward?

              Afterward? Afterward?
              The old Artaud
              is buried

dans le trou de la cheminée
qu'il tient de sa gencive froide
de ce jour où il fut tué !

Et après ?
Après ?
Après !
Il est ce trou sans cadre
que la vie voulut encadrer.
Parce qu'il n'est pas un trou
                    mais un nez
qui sut toujours trop bien renifler
le vent de l'apocalyptique
                    tête
qu'on pompe sur son cu serré,
et que le cu d'Artaud est bon
pour les souteneurs en miserere.

Et toi aussi tu as la gencive,
la gencive droite enterrée,
                    dieu,

toi aussi ta gencive est froide
depuis infiniment d'années
que tu m'envoyas ton cu inné
pour voir si j'allais être né
                    à la fin
depuis le temps que tu m'espérais

in the chimney hole
he owes to his cold gum
to the day when he was killed!

       And afterward?
       Afterward?
       Afterward!
He is this unframed hole
that life wanted to frame.
Because he is not a hole
       but a nose
that always knew all too well to sniff
the wind of the apocalyptic
       head
which they suck on his clenched ass,
and that Artaud's ass is good
for pimps in Miserere.

And you too you have your gum,
your right gum buried,
       god,

you too your gum is cold
for an infinity of years
since you sent me your innate ass
to see if I was going to be born
       at last
since the time you were waiting for me

en raclant
mon ventre d'absent.

menendi anenbi
embenda
tarch inemptle
o marchti rombi
tarch paiolt
a tinemptle
orch pendui
o patendi
a merchit
orch torpch
ta urchpt orchpt
ta tro taurch
campli
ko ti aunch
a ti aunch
aungbli

while scraping
my absentee belly.

**menendi anenbi
embenda
tarch inemptle
o marchti rombi
tarch paiolt
a tinemptle
orch pendui
o patendi
a merchit
orch torpch
ta urchpt orchpt
ta tro taurch
campli
ko ti aunch
a ti aunch
aungbli**

Centre mère et patron-minet

CENTER-MOTHER AND BOSS-PUSSY

Je parle le totem muré

car le totem mural est tel
que les formations visqueuses
de l'être
ne peuvent plus l'enfourcher de près.

C'est sexe carne
ce totem refoulé,

c'est une viande
de répulsion abstruse
ce squelette
qu'on ne peut
mâtiner,

ni de mère, ni
de père inné,

n'étant pas
la viande minette

I talk the enwalled totem

for the wall totem is such
that the viscous formations
of being
can no longer straddle it up close

It's old bag sex
this repressed totem,

it's a meat
of abstruse repulsion
this skeleton
that we can't
crossbreed,

neither with mother, nor
with innate father,

not being
the pussy meat

qu'on copule
à patron-minet.

Or la panse
n'etait pas affrétée
quand totem
entra dans l'histoire
pour en décourager
                l'entrée.

Et il fallut ventre à ventre cogner
chaque mère qui voulait pénétrer

chatte-mite en patron-minet

dans l'exsangue tube insurgé

comme au centre
de la panacée :

that we copulize[*]
at peep o'day.

Now the paunch
was not freighted
when totem
entered history
in order to discourage
　　　　　　　the entering.

And it was crucial belly to belly to bang
each mother who wanted to penetrate

pussy-toady[*] on boss-pussy

into the insurgent exsanguine tube

as at the center
of the panacea:

chatte-mite et patron-minet
sont les deux vocables salauds
que père et mère ont
                    inventés

pour jouir de lui au plus gros.

Qui ca, lui ?

Totem étranglé,

comme un membre dans une poche
que la vie *froche*
                    de si près,

qu'à la fin le totem muré
crèvera le ventre de naître

à travers la piscine enflée
du sexe de la mère ouverte

par la clef de **patron-minet.**

pussy-toady and boss-pussy
are the two sluttish vocables
that father and mother
               invented

to get the crudest pleasure out of him.

Who that, him?

Strangled totem,

like a member in a pocket
that life *frockets*[*]
             so close,

that in the end the enwalled totem
will burst the belly of birthing

through the swollen piscina
of the mother's sex organ opened

by **boss-pussy's** key.

Insulte à l'inconditionné

Insult to
the Unconditioned

C'est par la barbaque,
la sale barbaque
que l'on exprime

le,

qu'on ne sait pas

que

se placer hors

pour être sans,

avec, —

la barbaque
bien crottée et mirée
dans le cu d'une poule
morte et désirée.

It's through third-rate meat,
dirty third-rate meat
that we express

        the,

that we do not know

        that

        placing ourselves outside

        so as to be without,

        with, —

third-rate meat
really befouled and mirrored
in the ass of a tart
dead and desired.

Désirée, dis-je,
mais sans juter
des esquilles
blanches, lapées,

          (mornes de morve
          la salive)

          la salive
          de son dentier.

Avec la barbaque
qu'on se débarrasse
des **rats** de **l'inconditionné**.

Qui n'ont jamais senti
          que

          la non-forme,

          le hors-lieu
de la rogne sans condition,
appelée *le sans-condition*,

l'interférence de l'action,

le transfert par déportation;

le rétablissement hors coupure,

Desired, say I,
but without juicing off
white, lapped up
bone splinters,

       (buttes of mucous
       the saliva)

       the saliva
       from her false teeth.

With third-rate meat
let's get rid of
the **rats** of **the unconditioned**.

Who have never felt
       that

       the non-form

       the outside-place
of the foul temper without condition
called *the without-condition,*

the interference of action,

the transfer by deportation;

the reestablishment outside incision,

la coupure des colmatations;

l'assise enfin
dans le non hors,

l'imposition du dehors qui dort,
comme un dedans, éclaté des latrines
du canal où l'on chie la mort,

ne valent pas les desquamations
du con d'une moniche morte

quand la boniche qui le porte
pisse en arc-boutant
son pis

pour traverser
la syphilis.

the cutting of clogations;[*]

in short the foundation
in the non-outside,

the imposition of the outside which sleeps,
like an inside, burst from the latrines
of the canal where we shit death,

**are not worth the desquamations
from the cunt of a dead tench**[*]

**when the wench who bears it
pisses while buttressing
her tit**

**in order to cross
syphilis.**

L'Exécration
du père-mère

Execration of the Father-Mother

L'intelligence est venue après la sottise, laquelle l'a toujours sodomisée de près, — **ET APRÈS.**

Ce qui donne une idée de l'infini trajet.

Intelligence came after stupidity,
which had always sodomized it closely, —
AND THEN.

Which gives an idea of the infinite journey.

D'une préméditation de non-être,
d'une criminelle incitation de peut-être
est venue la réalité,
comme du hasard qui la forniquait.

From a premeditation of non-being,
from a criminal incitement of may-be
came reality,
as from chance which was fornicating it.

Je te condamne parce que tu sais
    pourquoi... je te condamne, —

et moi, je ne le sais pas.

I condemn you because you know
  why... I condemn you, —

and me, I don't know why.

Ce n'est pas un esprit qui a fait les choses,

It is not a spirit which has made things,

mais un corps, lequel pour être avait besoin de
crapuler,
avec sa verge à bonder son nez.

klaver striva
cavour tavina
scaver kavina
okar triva.

but a body, which in Order to be needed to
                                   wallow in vice,
with its penis for cramming its nose.

klaver striva
cavour tavina
scaver kavina
okar triva.

Pas de philosophie, pas de question, pas d'être,
pas de néant, pas de refus, pas de peut-être,

et pour le reste

crotter, crotter;

**ÔTER LA CROÛTE
DU PAIN BROUTÉ;**

No philosophy, no question, no being,
no nothingness, no refusal, no may-be,

as for the rest

to crap, to crap;

**STRIP THE CRUST
FROM THE BROWSED BREAD;**

ignobles déprédations
d'avinés dans les ciboires et les psautiers,
le vin des messes,
les crécelles des bonzes tartriques,
sortis innés d'un mamtram faussé,
tartre encroûtée d'un ancien crime,
latrines de sublimité !

l'heure approche où le puisatier qu'on déféqua
  dans les poubelles baptismales des bénitiers,
se rendra compte qu'il était moi.

ignoble depredations
of winos in the ciboria and the psalters,
the wine of the Masses,
the rattles of tartaric bonzes,
emerged innate from a warped mamtram,[*]
encrusted tartar of an ancient crime,
latrines of sublimity!

the hour draws near when the well driller who
  was defecated into the baptismal garbage cans
of holy water basins, will realize that he was me.

Or, je le sais.

Now, I know this.

Et ce fut toujours vidange pour ange,

And it was always drainage for angels,

et ma vidange passa la leur,
le jour où
forcé de sarcler dans les gommes syphilisées
d'une crasse depuis toujours constituée,
je compris que le sarclé c'était moi, —
et que vous défèque ce qu'on a défèqué,
si l'on ne prend pas
très à l'avance
la précaution de syphiliser

la verge abcès
DANS LA RENIFLE DU MUFLE
DE LA VOLONTÉ.

and my drainage surpassed theirs,
the day when
forced to hoe in the syphilitic resins
of a filth organized from the very beginning,
I understood that what was hoed was me, —
and that you defecate what they have defecated,
if they do not take
well in advance
the precaution to syphilize

the penis abscess
IN THE SNIFF OF THE MUZZLE
OF THE WILL.

Et que le plat s'allume en volume,
car le plat n'a pas de volume,
et c'est le volume qui est le plat;

le volume mange le plat
qui tourne de tous côtés pour ça.

And let flatness light up in volume,
for the flat has no volume,
and it is the volume which is the flat;

the volume eats the flat,
which turns on all sides because of that.

La breloque interne
était que
le partant qui est
toujours là

ne peut
bien se supporter
là

que
parce que
l'immobile
le porte

en fondant
toujours

le portant qui est
de toujours,

qu'il emporte

depuis toujours.

The internal watch charm
was that
the departer who is
always there

can
bear being
there

only
because
the unmoved
bears him

by always
melting

the bearer who
always is,

who it has been bearing away

from the very beginning.

Les esprits se procurent une minute
    d'intelligence
en me plongeant, moi, dans un bas-fond
    qu'ils se procurent
par absence de nourriture ou d'opium
    dans mon bedon,
maelström sur maelström de fond (de culture de
    par le fond),

après quoi ils retournent à leur ancestrale
    putréfaction.

Spirits procure for themselves an instant of
    intelligence
by plunging me, me, into a lower depth
    which they procure for themselves
through the absence of nourishment or opium
    in my potbelly,
maelstrom upon maelstrom of depth (of culture
    by way of the bottom),

after which they return to their ancestral
    putrefaction.

Si je me réveille tous les matins avec autour de moi
cette épouvantable odeur de foutre,
ce n'est pas que j'ai été succubé par les esprits de
l'au-delà, —

mais que les hommes de ce monde-ci
se passent le mot dans leur « perisprit » :

frottement de leurs couilles pleines,
sur le canal de leur anus
bien caressé et bien saisi,
afin de me pomper la vie.

If I wake up every morning surrounded by
this appalling odor of jism,
it is not because I have been succubused by the
spirits of the beyond, —

but because the men of this world here
pass the word around in their "perisprit":*

**rubbing of their full balls,
along the canal of their anus
nicely caressed and nicely grasped,
in order to pump out my life.**

« C'est que votre sperme est très bon,
m'a dit un jour
un flic au Dôme
qui se posait en connaisseur,
et quand on est « si bon »,
« si bon », dame,
on surpaye
son renom. »

Car probablement il en sortait
de ce sperme, si bon,
si bon;
et il l'avait baratté et sucé
à l'instar de
toute la terre,
tout le long de la nuit passée.

"It's that your sperm is very good,
a cop from the Dome
said to me one day
who set himself up as a connoisseur,
and when one is 'so good,'
'so good,' by god
one pays too much
for fame."

For probably he emerged from it
from this sperm, so good,
so good;
and he had churned and sucked it
like everyone
else in the world
the whole last night.

Et je sentis son âme virer,
ET JE LE VIS VERDIR DES PAUPIÈRES,
passer du copinage à la peur,

car il sentit que j'allais cogner.

And I saw his soul veer,
AND I SAW HIS EYELIDS TURN VERDIGRIS,
passing from chumminess to fear,

for he felt that I was going to strike.

Pas de tutoiement, ni de copinage,
jamais avec moi,
pas plus dans la vie que dans la pensée.

Et je ne sais pas si ce n'est pas en rêve
    que j'entends la fin de sa phrase :
« et quand on est si bon, si bon, dame, on
    surpaye son renom. »

No first name basis, nor chumminess,
never with me,
no more in life than in thought.

And I don't know if it isn't in a dream that
    I heard the end of his phrase:
"and when one is so good, so good, by god,
    one pays too much for fame."

Drôle de rêve où le squelette
de l'église et de la police
se tutoyaient
dans l'*arsenic* de ma liqueur séminale.

Car la vieille complainte revenait
de l'histoire du vieil Artaud assassiné
dans l'autre vie,
et qui n'entrera plus dans celle-ci.

Mais est-ce que je n'y suis pas entré
dans cette foutue branleuse vie
depuis cinquante ans que je suis né.

Weird dream where the skeleton
of the church and the police
were on a first name basis
in the *arsenic* of my seminal liquor.

For the old lament was coming back
from the story of the old Artaud assassinated
in the other life,
and who will not again enter this one.

But haven't I entered it
entered this fucked-up jerk-off life
in the fifty years since I've been born.

P.-S. — C'est une complainte que l'on récitait
   il n'y a pas encore six siècles dans les lycées
   de l'Afghanistan où Artaud s'orthographiait
   arto: *a. r. t. o.*
La même complainte se retrouve dans les vieilles
   légendes mazdéennes ou étrusques et dans des
   passages du Popol-Vuh.

P.S. — It's a lament that was recited not quite
six centuries ago in the high schools
of Afghanistan where Artaud was spelled
arto: a.r.t.o.
The same lament is found in old Mazdean or
Etruscan legends and in passages
of the Popol Vuh.

Aliénation
et Magie Noire

Alienation
and Black Magic

Les asiles d'aliénés sont des réceptacles
        de magie noire conscients et prémédités,

et ce n'est pas seulement que les médecins
        favorisent la magie par leurs thérapeutiques
        intempestives et hybrides,
c'est qu'ils en font.

S'il n'y avait pas eu de médecins
il n'y aurait jamais eu de malades,
pas de squelettes de morts
malades à charcuter et dépiauter,
car c'est par les médecins et non par les malades
        que la société a commencé.

Ceux qui vivent, vivent des morts.
Et il faut aussi que la mort vive;
et il n'y a rien comme un asile d'aliénés pour
        couver doucement la mort, et tenir en
        couveuse des morts.

Cela a commencé 4000 ans avant Jésus-christ
cette thérapeutique de la mort lente,

Insane asylums are conscious and premeditated
    receptacles of black magic,

and it is not only that doctors encourage magic
    with their inopportune and hybrid
    therapies,
it is how they use it.

If there had been no doctors
there would never have been patients,
no skeletons of the diseased
dead to butcher and flay,
for it is through doctors and not through
    patients that society began.

Those who live, live off the dead.
And it is likewise necessary that death live;
and there is nothing like an insane asylum for
    gently incubating death, and for keeping the
    dead in incubators.

It began 4000 years before Jesus christ
this therapy of slow death,

et la médecine moderne, complice en cela
de la plus sinistre et crapuleuse magie,
passe ses morts à l'électro-choc ou à
l'insulino-thérapie afin de bien chaque jour
vider ses haras d'hommes de leur moi,
et de les présenter ainsi vides,
ainsi fantastiquement
disponibles et vides,
aux obscènes sollicitations anatomiques et
atomiques
de l'état appelé **Bardo**, livraison du **barda**
de vivre aux exigences du non-moi.

Le Bardo est l'affre de mort dans lequel
le moi tombe en flaque,
et il y a dans l'électro-choc un état flaque
par lequel passe tout traumatisé,
et qui lui donne, non plus à cet instant
de connaître, mais d'affreusement et
déséspérement méconnaître ce qu'il fut,
quand il était soi, quoi, loi, moi, roi, toi,
zut et ÇA.

J'y suis passé et ne l'oublierai pas.

La magie de l'électro-choc draine un râle,
elle plonge le commotionné dans ce râle
par lequel on quitte la vie.

Or, les électro-chocs du Bardo ne furent jamais
une expérience, et râler dans l'électro-choc du
Bardo, comme dans le Bardo de l'électro-choc,
c'est déchiqueter une expérience sucée par
les larves du non-moi, et que l'homme
ne retrouvera pas.

Au milieu de cette palpitation et de cette
respiration de tous les autres qui assiègent celui

and modern medicine, an accomplice in this of
the most sinister and crapulous magic,
subjects its dead to electroshock or to insulin
therapy so as daily to throughly empty its
stud farms of men of their egos,
and to expose them thus empty,
thus fantastically
available and empty,
to the obscene anatomical and atomic
solicitations
of the state called **Bardo**, delivery of the **full kit**
for living to the demands of the non-ego.

Bardo is the death throes in which the ego falls
in a puddle,
and there is in electroshock a puddle state
through which everyone traumatized passes,
and which causes him, no longer at this moment
to know, but to dreadfully and desperately
misjudge what he was, when he was
himself, his own elf, his fief, wife, life,
tripe, damnit and THAT.[*]

I went through it and I won't forget it.

The magic of electroshock drains a death rattle,
it plunges the shocked into that rattle with
which we leave life.

But, the electroshocks of Bardo were never an
experiment, and to death rattle in the
electroshock of Bardo, as in the Bardo of
electroshock, is to mangle an experiment
sucked by the larvae of the non-ego, and
that man will not recapture.

In the midst of this palpitation and this
respiration of all the others who

qui, comme disent les Mexicains, raclant pour
l'entamer l'ecorce de sa râpe, *coule de tous
côtés sans loi.*

La médecine soudoyée ment chaque fois qu'elle
présente un malade guéri par les
introspections électriques de sa méthode,
je n'ai vu, moi, que des terrorisés de la méthode,
incapables de retrouver leur moi.

Qui a passé par l'électro-choc du Bardo, et le Bardo
de l'électro-choc, ne remonte plus jamais
de ses ténèbres, et la vie a baissé d'un cran.
J'y ai connu ces moléculations souffle après souffle
du râle des authentiques agonisants.

Ce que les Tarahumaras du Mexique appellent
le crachat de la râpe, l'escarbille du charbon
sans dents.

Perte d'un pan de l'euphorie première qu'on eut
un jour à se sentir vivant, déglutinant et
mastiquant.

C'est ainsi que l'électro-choc comme le Bardo crée
des larves, il fait de tous les états pulvérisés
du patient, de tous les faits de son passé des
larves inutilisables pour le présent et qui
ne cessent plus d'assiéger le present.

Or, je le répète, le Bardo c'est la mort, et **la mort
n'est qu'un état de magie noire qui
n'existait pas il n'y a pas si longtemps.**

besiege the one who, as the Mexicans say,
scraping to broach the bark with his grater,
flows lawlessly from all sides.

Bribed medicine lies each time that it presents
a patient cured by the electrical
introspections of its method, as for me,
I've seen only those who have been terrorized by
the method, incapable of recovering their egos.

Who has gone through the electroshock of Bardo,
and the Bardo of electroshock, never climbs
up again from its tenebrae, and life has
slipped a notch.
I've known there these moleculations breath upon
breath of the death rattle of authentically
agonizing people.

What the Tarahumaras of Mexico call the spittle
of the grater, the cinder of toothless coal.

Loss of a slap of the first euphoria that you had
one day feeling yourself alive, swallowing[*]
and chewing.

It is thus that electroshock like Bardo creates larvae,
it turns all the patient's pulverized states, all
the facts of his past into larvae which are
unusable in the present yet which never
cease beseiging the present.

Now, I repeat, Bardo is death, and **death is only a
state of black magic which did not exist
not so long ago.**

Créer ainsi artificiellement la mort comme la
        médecine actuelle l'entreprend c'est
        favoriser un reflux du néant qui n'a jamais
        profité à personne,
mais dont certains profiteurs prédestinés de
        l'homme se repaissent depuis longtemps.

En fait, depuis un certain point du temps.

Lequel ?

Celui où il fallut choisir entre renoncer à être
        homme ou devenir un aliéné évident.

Mais quelle garantie les aliénés évidents de ce
        monde ont-ils d'être soignés par
        d'authentiques vivants ?

        **farfadi
        ta azor
        tau ela
        auela
        a
        tara
        ila**

        F I N

To thus create death artificially as present-day
medicine attempts to do is to encourage a
reflux of the nothingness which has never
been to anyone's benefit,
but off which certain predestined human profiteers
have been eating their fill for a long time.

Actually, since a certain point in time.

Which one?

That point when it was necessary to choose between
renouncing being a man and becoming an
obvious madman.

But what guarantee do the obvious madmen of this
world have of being nursed by the
authentically living?

**farfadi
ta azor
tau ela
auela
a
tara
ila**

T H E   E N D

Une page blanche pour séparer le texte du livre
qui est fini de tout le grouillement du Bardo
qui apparaît dans les limbes de l'électro-
choc.

Et dans ces limbes une typographie spéciale,
laquelle est là pour abjecter dieu, mettre en
retrait les paroles verbales auxquelles une
valeur spéciale a voulu être attribuée.

ANTONIN ARTAUD
12 janvier 1948

A blank page to separate the text of the book, which
is finished from all the swarming of Bardo
which appeared in the limbo of electro-
shock.

And in this limbo a special typography, which is
there to abject god, to background the
verbal words to which one wanted to
attribute a special value.

ANTONIN ARTAUD
12 January 1948

tu t'en vas,
dit l'immonde tutoiement du Bardo,
et tu es toujours là,

you're leaving, kid,
says the scummy familiarity of Bardo,
and you're still there,

tu n'es plus là
mais rien ne te quitte,
tu as tout conservé
sauf toi-même
et que t'importe puisque
le monde
est là.

Le
monde,
mais ce n'est plus moi.
Et que t'importe,
dit le Bardo,
c'est moi.

you're no longer there
but nothing leaves you,
you've kept everything
except yourself
and what's it to you since
the world
is there.

The
world,
but it's no longer me.
And what's it to you, kid,
says Bardo,
it's me.

P.-S. — J'ai à me plaindre d'avoir dans l'électro-choc
rencontré des morts que je n'aurais pas voulu
voir.

Les mêmes,
que ce livre imbécile appelé
Bardo Todol
draine et propose depuis un peu plus de quatre
mille ans.

Pourquoi ?

Je demande simplement:
Pourquoi ? ...

P.S. — I want to complain about having met in
electroshock dead people whom I wouldn't
have chosen to see.

The same ones,
whom this imbecilic book called
Bardo Todol
has been draining and proposing for a little more
than four thousand years.

Why?

I simply ask:
Why? ...

NOTES BY CLAYTON ESHLEMAN

The poems, or texts, that make up the complete work were written between July and September, 1946. It is the first major work that Artaud started and completed after his release from Rodez, and on this level, it may be thought of as a bristling declaration that he is back. The work was originally published as a book by Bordas, in January, 1948, with eight drawings by Artaud. As in the case of many texts created after leaving Rodez, *Artaud the Mômo* was begun in notebooks (the "dossier" of worksheets takes up 124 pages in *Œuvres complètes*, XII), then dictated to an assistant, after which it was corrected in typescript and in several sets of proofs. *Artaud the Mômo* is probably Artaud's most honed and polished work.

"Mômo" is Marseilles slang for simpleton, or village idiot, and as we understand it, "Artaud the Mômo" is the phoenix-like figure which rose from the ashes of the death of "the old Artaud" probably in electroshock in Rodez in 1943 or 1944. "The Return of Artaud, the Mômo" might be understood as the return of Artaud, now as a Mômo, to the world of imagination, as well as to literary life in Paris. One must also take into consideration this word's relation to the Greek god of mockery and raillery, Momus, said by Hesiod to be the son of Sleep and Night, the nocturnal voice of Hermes, bearing in his hand a crotalum (in contrast to a caduceus). Because of the rich associations of Mômo/Momus, we have decided not to translate the word. As in the case of the word "negritude" in the work of Aime Césaire, Artaud seems to have possessed the word and, in poetry, made it his own.

p. 9: "It's the penetral... anayor": This quatrain contains a complex web of sound and association, some of which is untranslatable. Soundwise, there is the play on "toile," "pentrale," "poile," "voile," and "anale," as well as on "ou" which occurs four times. "Poil" (fur or hair) is normally masculine; here Artaud has feminized it, by adding an "e," so that it matches "toile" and "voile." It happens that "poile" does exist, as an archaic form of "poêle" (a toga, mantle, cloak, or pall). Since "poêle" is masculine, we should probably rule it out as the meaning of the (now) feminine "la poile." However, it is very tempting to accept the archaic and masculine "poile" as Artaud's intention, since as a "pall" it metaphorically rhymes with the web ("toile d'araignée") and, in its masculine form, "voile" as veil (in ontrast to the feminine meaning, sail). It is tempting to go for web, pall, and veil, which strongly evoke "the veil of Isis," or feminine mystery, which Artaud seems to be evoking in this quatrain (to some extent contradicted by the last line). However, there is no reason to assume that the usually quite precise Artaud became gender careless in this quatrain, so while we make a few adjustments to coax as much play out of the quatrain as possible, we respect the feminine pronouns.

"onor" appears to be old French for "honor." There is a slight possibility that Artaud had Onuris, a god from Upper Egypt in mind. "la plaque anale" (anal plate) is possibly explained by the following definition of a chastity belt (from *The Book of Lists*, Bantam, 1980): "a leather-covered iron hoop to which were attached a frontal plate with a saw-toothed slit and an anal plate, which had a small opening." While the "ana" of "anavou" picks up the "ana" in "anale," we also hear "a vous" in "avou" and, given our attempt to parallel the French "ou" sounds with "or" sounds in English, render it as "yor" (a playful contraction of "your").

p. 9: "old bag": A much-pondered solution for "carne," which the *Dictionnaire érotique* (Payot, 1993) defines as "femme, au sens de 'vieux cheval'; pejoratif traditionnel de la femme." The word, however, does not appear to be that simple, with Harraps defining it as: 1. (a) tough meat; (b) old horse; screw. 2. (a) bad-tempered person; (of man) cantankerous brute; (of woman) bitch; (b) wastrel, bad egg; (of woman) slut." The word's appearance in the poem, as "une carne," seems to register a kind of woman, rather than meat. However, in one of the early drafts for this section (*OC* XII, p. 116), Artaud replaces "viande" (meat) with "carne" in the line: "cette carne entre deux genoux," indicating that "carne" may be a substitute, in the section, for "viande." It appears to be impossible to translate "carne" in a single word as low-quality or tough meat. To try to do so is to be forced into such words as "gristle" or "mutton," for example, which signal meaning associations that are irrelevant. While "old bag" probably compromises to some extent the denotative density of "carne," it plays off "hole" and "palm" in fascinating ways.

p. 15: "alienage": A coined cognate for "alienage," which appears to have been coined, in French, by Artaud.

p. 31: "copulize": Based on "copule," coined by Artaud apparently off "copulation" (copulation).

p. 31: "pussy-toady": "chatte-mite" appears to be a cognate for the English "catamite" but this is not so. A "chattemite" is a sanctimonious person, a toady. By hyphenating "chatte-mite," Artaud emphasizes "chatte" (slang for "pussy").

p. 33: *"frockets"*: Based on *"froche,"* which appears to have been invented by Artaud. It plays off "poche" (pocket) in the line above, as well as off "toucher" (to touch) and "frôler" (to rub or brush).

p. 43: "clogation": Based on "colmatations," which appears to be an Artaud variation on "colmatage" (plugging, clogging).

p. 43: "tench": Archaic slang for "vagina." It is used here to match "moniche" (archaic thieves' slang for the same). "Moniche" rhymes with "boniche" in the same passage; thus our choice of "tench" to rhyme with "wench."

p. 61: "mamtram": Probably coined off "mantra," a sacred Sanskrit text or a Tantric spell. It is impossible to know if this is a mishearing on Artaud's part, or his play, possibly, on "mama" and "trame" (woof, plot). Artaud's work is furrowed with mommy plots.

p. 75: "perisprit": A rare synonym for the fluid envelope, or astral body, that in certain occult lore is believed to exist between the body and the spirit. Artaud must have spotted "père" (father) and "esprit" (spirit) in the word.

p. 93: "when he was himself... and THAT": Literally, this passage might have been translated as "when he was himself, what, law, me, king, you, damnit and THAT." Since all these words rhyme in French, we have given priority to the sound here.

p. 95: "swallowing": "déglutinant" seems to be based on "déglutiner" (and not on "déglutir," to swallow), a rare word that refers to removing bird lime (the "glu") from a bird's feathers, as an aspect of hunting. Since this word is juxtaposed with "mastiquant" (chewing), we translate it as "swallowing." The alternative would simply look bizarre, and obscure the obvious connection between swallowing and chewing.

Stephen Barber

Artaud's Last Work & Artaud the Mômo

Clayton Eshleman's translations of Antonin Artaud's work – the finest yet undertaken, and those that best seize the intensive furore and engulfing intricacy of that work – focus solely on Artaud's final period, from the last months of his three-year incarceration at the asylum of Rodez in southern France, and from the subsequent twenty-two months of his life back in Paris, after his release from that asylum, and extending until his death. That final period – from the early months of 1946 until the moment of Artaud's death on 4 March 1948 – is undoubtedly the richest, most productive phase of his work, and possesses a fury and discipline far beyond that of his work with the Surrealist movement in the 1920s and his Theatre of Cruelty project of the 1930s. It is the period when Artaud's preoccupations are at their most livid and confrontational, but also the period when he finally seizes control of his language, and wields a unique and astonishing corporeal poetry. It is also the period in which, after a decade of planning projects that were never realized, and a further decade of stultified asylum incarceration, Artaud finally unleashes his work in forms that its own volatile velocity serves to create: a series of major poetic works and a huge number of fragments, several recordings for radio transmission, and seventy or so large-scale drawings. There is no time remaining for linguistic frailty or for aesthetic hesitation in Artaud's last work: everything is projected from his body, immediately, simultaneously, infinitely. Over several decades of exacting work, from the 1970s to the 2000s, Eshleman – a prominent poet in his own right – translated all of Artaud's essential writings of that last period, from his major poetic works such as *Artaud the Mômo* and *Watchfiends and Rack Screams*, to his censored radio texts, to his writings on his drawings, and to his final fragments, publishing those translations in now-unavailable collections and in issues of the poetry magazine which he edited in that era, *Sulfur*.

Artaud's final period is the culmination of his life's work, but in a very particular, non-linear and even aberrant sense. It forms the intensification and projection of obsessions which are present in the very first of his writings as a young poet, thirty years earlier – above all, the desire for a new kind of human anatomy, and the reconfiguration or expunging of the mental world – but which are no longer cast in pre-ordained forms (such as those of the film synopsis or of the theatre manifesto which he had adopted in his work of the 1920s and 1930s), and instead are instilled within a pulsing, immediate poetry that struggles with itself, constantly remaking itself as a livid self-autopsying process. Following the collapse of his Theatre of Cruelty project in 1935, Artaud had embarked on a series of gruelling journeys that ended with his arrest and asylum incarceration in 1937: firstly to Mexico, to the village of Norogachic in the Tarahumara mountains, with the aim to take peyote and investigate the potential for a new culture of fire and corporeal transmutation; and then to Inishmore, one of the remote Aran Islands off the western coast of Ireland, where he intended to witness a literally apocalyptic event from the vantage-point of the huge pre-Christian hill-forts of that barren, wild island. The final period of his work forms the culmination of those journeys' headlong excavation into the boundaries of the human body and its culture. Finally, Artaud's last period is the terminal-point for his decade of asylum incarceration, in the sense of forming the negation and repudiation of what he viewed as society's forcible eradication of his work's virulence, notably through the near-fatal starvation and beatings he had endured at the third asylum, Ville-Evrard, and the series of fifty-one electroshock treatments he had received at the last asylum, Rodez, from its director, Gaston Ferdière, and his assistant, Jacques Latrémolière; the denunciation of what he had faced in the asylums remains a presence that constantly inflects and imparts an extreme combativeness to Artaud's final work.

Artaud has a distinctive set of preoccupations at the end of his life, which form the axis of the poetry, letters and fragments of his final period. Above all, for Artaud, the human body has become nullified and redundant – and must now be violently transformed, so that almost all of its organs are jettisoned (it was Artaud's call for a 'corps sans organes', notably in his texts for the radio-recording *To have done with the judgement of god* – translated in their entirety by Eshleman – that inspired the seminal theoretical work of the French philosophers Gilles Deleuze and Félix Guattari); Artaud imagines, plans and attempts to undertake that corporeal reactivation, through the medium of language. He relentlessly disassembles and probes the elements of his own damaged body and thereby generates an unprecedented poetry of human fragmentation. The natural world, too, has been contaminated and wastelanded, rendered synthetic and despoiled, for Artaud, and now needs to be imbued with a new ferocity and turbulence that allies it to his visions for the human body. All evidence of society, religion, sexuality and medicine is anathema to Artaud, and their erasure is an urgent demand of his final work; only his resuscitated body, and the world it engenders, will endure. Finally, Artaud's last period is profoundly preoccupied with death, as a state of black-magic bewitchment deployed by social power to maintain itself; although Artaud was only forty-nine years old at the moment of his release from Rodez, he anticipated his imminent death, or declared that it had already taken place. In newspaper interviews given during February 1948, Artaud imagined moments in human history when death had not existed, and insisted those moments could be revivified through the determination not to die, and through a creative regime of hammer-blows and knife-incisions exacted against society's henchmen and assassins. On the last night of his life, Artaud wrote in his final notebook that he had been: 'tipped over/into death,/ there where I ceaselessly eat/cock,/anus/and caca/at all my meals,/all those of THE CROSS.' His very last words detail his terminal confrontations with maleficent agents of society: 'the same individual/returns, then, each/morning (it's another)/to accomplish his/revolting, criminal/ and murderous, sinister/task which is to/maintain/a state of *bewitchment* in/me/and to continue to/render me/an eternally/bewitched man/etc etc'.[1]

Artaud moved across creative media in the final period of his life with extraordinary agility and a sense of oblivion directed towards the expectation that a poet need work only in one form. In the 1920s and 1930s, his work in cinema and theatre had been done on a sustained basis, only interrupted and stalled by the incessant financial obstacles to the accomplishment of his planned films and spectacles. His final work is undertaken in a different way: Artaud welds together his poems, his drawings and his sound-recordings, at speed, often so that they work in confrontation with one another. His primary medium at that time was that of the notebook, in which he inscribed textual fragments (some of them expanded or dictated into the form of major poetic works, as with *Artaud the Mômo*), notations about his preoccupations and daily life, work-in-progress towards the texts and screams he was preparing to record for radio transmission, and innumerable, densely rendered drawings of corporeal mutation, weapons and torture-instruments; sometimes, his notebooks are pierced-through, from cover to cover, with a constellation of blows from violently wielded pencil-points, pen-nibs or knife-blades, so that the pages and covers are stained with the traces of many fluids. The alacrity and ferocity with which Artaud wrote down his texts frequently tears-through or shreds the pages' thin paper. The three notebooks which Artaud prepared for his one public performance (alongside two private art-gallery readings) of the final period of his life – at the Vieux-Colombier theatre in January 1947 – are multiply overlayered, text upon text, as though the preparations for that unique performance (at which, on the night, Artaud discarded his notebooks and delivered an improvisation) required the obliteration of language itself and the annulling of representation. Artaud had begun using the medium of the notebook at the beginning of 1945, while still interned at the Rodez asylum, and continued deploying notebooks until the end of his life, by which time he had amassed a total of 406 notebooks. He bought the cheapest schoolchildren's notebooks, made of shoddy, discoloured wartime and immediate post-war paper, and jammed them, several at a time, into his jacket-pocket, folded vertically, on his journeys around Paris.

Artaud's way of working, after his release from Rodez in May 1946, demanded a mobile medium, which his notebooks provided. He lived, throughout his final twenty-two months, on the periphery of Paris, in a private convalescence-home in the industrial port-suburb of Ivry-sur-Seine (historically one of the most left-wing Parisian suburbs, from which a large contingent of fighters had left for the Spanish Civil War, ten years earlier); it had been a condition of his release from Rodez that he remained in an institution, although the Ivry clinic, where James Joyce's daughter Lucia had also been a patient, was a dilapidated and shambolic environment which accorded Artaud a high degree of freedom of movement. He would leave by metro-train for central Paris each morning, taking his notebooks-in-progress with him, and spent his days on the move, meeting friends (his closest companions of the period were the actor Roger Blin, and the writers Arthur Adamov and Marthe Robert, all of whom he had known before his incarceration, alongside new, younger friends such as Paule Thévenin and Colette Thomas), writing alone in the cafes of St Germain-des-Prés, especially the Flore, or making the journey up to Montmartre in search of laudanum, heroin and chloral hydrate. He worked incessantly throughout the course of each day, often stopping in the street and standing upright as he inscribed texts into his notebooks, or working on metro-trains and buses; he would then take the last metro of the evening back to Ivry-sur-Seine. A young tubercular poet, Jacques Prevel, accompanied Artaud on many of his urban trajectories, and noted every detail in his journal (published in 1974, and re-issued, expanded, in 1994, as *En Compagnie d'Antonin Artaud*), providing an exhaustive record, often hour by hour, of Artaud's working process during much of his final period.

Several months after arriving at the convalescence home, Artaud had requested that its director allow him to distance himself from its other patients, by moving into a derelict, two-room pavilion on the edge of its extensive, wooded grounds. Photographs of the eighteenth-century pavilion show its location as being alongside the high boundary-wall of the grounds, close to the main avenue of Ivry-sur-Seine (in an area that, following the convalescence home's demolition, became a public park); the pavilion's main room had an immense fireplace. Alongside his notebook-writings and notebook-drawings undertaken on his journeys around Paris, and during visits to friends' apartments, Artaud also worked extensively in his pavilion, in the mornings and at night. He had always dictated the final versions of his books, whenever he could persuade his publishers to provide him with a secretary or assistant; in 1933, the final version of his account of the life of the Roman Emperor, Heliogabalus, had been entirely dictated from working-notes. He continued this approach in the final period of his life, in collaboration with Paule Thévenin, who became a close friend for Artaud, performed for his radio work, and would edit the twenty-six-volume edition of his *Oeuvres complètes* for the publisher Gallimard after Artaud's death. In particular, many of the texts from the *Interjections* section of his most ambitious poetic work of that era, *Watchfiends and Rack Screams*, were dictated over a four-month period, around the end of 1946, for that book-project commissioned by the publisher Louis Broder, then passed-on to another publisher, K (and not eventually published until 1978). Taking dictation from Artaud was a demanding process, since he expectorated his intricate texts, partly composed from invented glossolaliac elements of language, and cut by long silences, while lying in bed in the mornings, often drinking coffee and chewing his breakfast at the same time; several transcribers, including the young editor (and future filmmaker) Chris Marker, lasted only for short periods of time, before a brisk, undaunted secretary, Luciane Abiet, took over. In 1993, Luciane Abiet gave an interview for a documentary film on Artaud's final period, *La véritable histoire d'Artaud le Mômo* (directed by Gérard Mordillat and Jérôme Prieur) in which she described her morning visits to Artaud's pavilion for the dictation of the *Interjections* texts, and the difficulties and near-impossibilities she faced in mediating the volatile, scrambled oral-content from Artaud's mouth into a written transcription.

Most of Artaud's large-scale drawings were also undertaken at his Ivry-sur-Seine pavilion; the drawings are mostly portraits – astonishing facial excavations and anatomical reconfigurations – of friends and visitors to the pavilion. The poem *The Human Face*, on those large-scale drawings, was written for a pamphlet that accompanied the sole exhibition of Artaud's drawings during his lifetime, at the Galerie Pierre in July 1947, while *Ten Years that Language has been Gone* focuses instead on the smaller drawings, intersected with texts, that Artaud inscribed in his 406 notebooks; Eshleman translated both texts.

In the final months of his life, from the late summer of 1947 onwards, Artaud was largely incapacitated by illness, addiction and exhaustion, and his pavilion became the main arena for his work. He prepared and recorded the last of his three projects for radio, *To have done with the judgement of god* (a work composed of poetic texts, screams and cries, and percussive elements) which he viewed as the ultimate manifestation of his preoccupations, but its abrupt censorship, by the director of the French national radio station, for reasons of blasphemy and obscenity, disheartened him; he wrote to his friend, the writer and publisher Jean Paulhan, on 12 February 1948: 'LAMENTABLE that the recording wasn't transmitted. You would have finally seen what the Theatre of Cruelty could have been.'[2] Although he still made occasional journeys into central Paris, Artaud remained mostly fixed in his pavilion, writing ever-more skeletal, violent and corrosive notebook-fragments, and still immersed in his reconfiguration of the human anatomy and of death, over the final weeks of his life.

Eshleman's translations of Artaud's final period refocused and transformed the perception of Artaud's work for its English-language readership on their initial publications, and still do so, even more acutely, in Diaphanes' new editions. Eshleman's translations, for the first time, present Artaud in English in an authentic form, rendered both with great creativity and erudition, and with an intricate and ferocious corporeality that matches Artaud's own; Eshleman translated Artaud with a comprehensive scholarly knowledge of the entirety of his work and of its multiple forms – the result of many decades of sustained engagement. Strangely, for a figure of Artaud's vast stature and influence, the English-language translations of his work over the past sixty or more years have never otherwise reached the affinitive and sensorial intensity that Eshleman achieves. From the first translation of Artaud in 1958, the Grove Press edition of *The Theatre and its Double* – and passing through Jack Hirshman's City Lights *Artaud Anthology* of 1965, the British publisher John Calder's volumes of 1968-74, Susan Sontag's edition of *Selected Writings* in 1976, and more recent publications – Artaud has often been banalized, sent askew, or has simply suffered the process of mis-representation he most feared and attacked. Hirschman's edition – a massive seller in the late 1960s, and the previous volume with a particular focus on Artaud's late work – demonstrates the combination of idiosyncrasy, misplaced enthusiasm and sheer ill-informedness that has often plagued English-language

translations of Artaud. On receiving Hirschman's manu-
script (the work of numerous translators) in 1964, its pub-
lisher, Lawrence Ferlinghetti, who had commissioned the
anthology, wrote to Hirschman: 'I don't really understand
how you operate... I do not understand your criteria for
the *order*, or sequence, of the contents as a whole. It's not
chronological, is it? What is it?'(3); Artaud's close collab-
orator Paule Thévenin complained in a letter to Ferling-
hetti: 'The more deeply I look into the work Hirschman
has done, the more furious I become... How on earth, to
be frank about this, could you have put your trust in a
person who doesn't speak a word of French and also
doesn't understand a word of it?'4.Even so, prior to Eshle-
man's translations, it was Hirschman's anthology that had
provoked and actively perplexed – sometimes propelling
them towards the original French – its hundreds of thou-
sands of readers, such as Patti Smith, over several decades.

Since 1987, Artaud's drawings and notebooks have
been exhibited many times, at Paris's Centre Georges
Pompidou, New York's Museum of Modern Art, Vienna's
Museum of Modern Art, and London's Cabinet Gallery,
also transforming and realigning the perception of his
work. The notebooks' curator at the Bibliothèque Natio-
nale de France, Guillaume Fau, has accomplished invalu-
able work in making them accessible and in envisioning
their eventual digitisation. The series of events at Cabi-
net Gallery, Whitechapel Gallery and Visconti Studio
in London in 2018 (marking the seventieth anniversary
of Artaud's death and the end of decades of constrictive
copyright controls and bitter feuds among Artaud's heirs)
demonstrated the immense and interconnected span of
Artaud's work – poetry, sound, film, art – for the first time.
This series embodies that same aim of projecting the infi-
nite span and profound strata of Artaud's work, evident
most tangibly in its last moments, and for English-lan-
guage readers in Eshleman's magnificent translations.

Artaud the Mômo is Artaud's most extraordinary poetic
work from the brief final phase of his life, extending from

his return to Paris in 1946 after nine years of incarceration in psychiatric institutions, to his death in 1948. The work is an all-engulfing anatomical excavation carried through in vocal language, envisioning unprecedented gestural futures for the human body in its splintered fragments. With deeply black humour, Artaud also illuminates his own status as the scorned, Marseille-born child-fool, the "Mômo" (a self-naming that fascinated Jacques Derrida in his writings on this work). Artaud moves between extreme irreligious obscenity and delicate evocations both of his immediate corporeal perception and his sense of solitude. The book's five-part sequence ends with Artaud's caustic denunciation of psychiatric institutions and of the very concept of madness itself, in the text *Alienation and Black Magic* which he also recorded for radio transmission on 16 July 1946.

Artaud the Mômo was written in the months following Artaud's release from the asylum of Rodez on 25 May 1946 and overnight journey by train to Paris, and the work announces his combative, self-willed 'return' to the city which he had left in August 1937 to travel to Inishmore, to witness his anticipated Apocalypse (expected by Artaud to engulf Paris in fire, cacophony and destruction). Artaud had passed through Paris several times while incarcerated, spending time for assessment by Jacques Lacan at the Sainte-Anne asylum in central Paris and also interned for several wartime years at the Ville-Evrard asylum beyond Paris's eastern periphery, but those were journeys in which his figure was clothed in an asylum uniform and was accompanied by brutal guards whom he accused of beating him and kicking him in the testicles during his many transfers between asylums. His return to Paris of 1946, by contrast, was in fierce autonomy.

    Artaud the Mômo was not published for a year and a half after its completion, delayed by disputes about its design as well as by the conditions of material scarcity in Paris in that post-war moment. The book appeared in an edition of 355 copies (around the same number of copies as most of Artaud's books of that era, with only his essay on Van Gogh appearing in a larger edition, of 2,000 copies), each copy containing reproductions of eight drawings by Artaud, taken from his notebooks. The book's publication is uniquely documented through twelve letters which its publisher, Pierre Bordas, preserved and donated to the Bibliothèque Nationale de France in 1981, despite the vitriol and abuse against him which those letters held. None of Bordas's letters to Artaud survived; throughout his life, Artaud never preserved the letters sent to him. Bordas also donated the set of proofs for *Artaud the Mômo*, corrected by Artaud on 18-19 April 1947 using several different coloured inks; it's clear he became infuriated at one point, on the final page, and lacerates the proofs' page with his pen's nib or another implement, creating voids in the paper.

Artaud's letters to Bordas on the publication of *Artaud the Mômo* give deep insights into the ways in which he conceived of the public audience for his work, as well as into his preoccupations during his life's final years. Bordas was in his mid thirties at the time when he published *Artaud the Mômo*, and he was also at that moment one of the first publishers of Samuel Beckett, as well as the instigator of many collaborations in book form between poets and artists, including those formerly associated with the Surrealist group; Bordas soon switched his focus completely (undoubtedly in part through his volatile rapports with Artaud and his other authors) and moved for several decades into scholarly textbook and dictionary publishing, though his final publishing projects of the 1990s returned to experiments in art.

Artaud's first correspondence with Bordas (a card rather than a letter), from 26 December 1946, reveals that Bordas's first plan for *Artaud the Mômo* was that it would take the form of a collaboration between Artaud and Pablo Picasso. Artaud was on cordial terms with Picasso, but it's evident that Picasso was either disinterested in collaborating with him, or else too preoccupied by other projects; Artaud asserts that he has made five appointments to meet

Picasso at his studio, and Picasso has been absent on every occasion. Artaud is still willing to pursue the book in that collaborative form, telling Bordas: 'I'll do what I can.'[5]

By the time of Artaud's next communication with Bordas, in a letter of 6 February 1947, it's clear that Bordas's desired collaboration between Artaud and Picasso will not happen. Artaud now wants to use his own drawings in the book; he denounces the 'incompetence' of Picasso and asserts: 'Picasso could never understand me as I understand myself.' (Picasso did eventually illustrate a book of Artaud's notebook writings from his final period, but not until 1958, after Artaud's death.) Artaud insists that including his own drawings will create: 'work that will be *astonishing* in its innovativeness', and he attempts to persuade Bordas that his own current notoriety (following his lecture-performance of the previous month at the Vieux-Colombier theatre) will ensure good sales of the book: 'Don't forget that at the Vieux-Colombier they had 1,000 people in an auditorium seating 350 and refused entry to 400 people and that wasn't due to the glory of my name.' Now the book will be an amalgam of his poems and drawings: 'I propose to you that I will illustrate my 5 poems with a *dozen* drawings representing totems... mysterious operating machines.'[6] He didn't succeed in convincing Bordas, who reduced Artaud's advance payment and royalties percentage in the contract for the book, to reflect Picasso's non-participation.

Artaud's next two letters to Bordas in April-May 1947 form demands for extra money following the advance payment (30,000 francs) which he had received on his contract's signature. Artaud tells Bordas he is now planning a long journey (one he did not make) to Corsica and then North Africa: 'I'll therefore be staying for a long time... in a location most likely *without a postal service.*'[7] Bordas declined to pay Artaud the requested extra money. As a result, Artaud attempted to sell the rights to *Artaud the Mômo* also to another publisher, the young Lyon-based publisher Marc Barbezat who had published Jean Genet's first novels and was planning to publish texts by

Artaud in his large-format magazine, 'L'Arbalète', writing to Barbezat on 6 May 1947: 'I'm mad with rage against the 3 Paris publishers with whom I've agreed contracts: Gaston Gallimard, Pierre Bordas, Pierre Loeb and whom I consider to be troublemakers, dishonest people and *also bad workers*.'[8] Artaud eventually went ahead with the publication of *Artaud the Mômo* with Bordas, but demanded that the book's typography should resemble that used by Barbezat for 'LArbalète', with large, thick and well-spaced characters. He also demands the use of luxurious matte paper of a kind that was difficult for Bordas to access in that era of Paris's acute austerity. In a letter of 6 June 1947, Artaud insists: 'so that will make for sumptuousness and will enhance a deluxe book'; in the same letter, he denounces Bordas's printers for the quality of the proofs Artaud has been sent, complaining that his *Artaud the Mômo* poems are 'too revolutionary' for the printers and that they have tried to sabotage them.[9]

The selection of drawings to be reproduced within *Artaud the Mômo* is the focus of the following letters of 6 August and 27 September 1947. At first, Artaud attempts to delegate the choice of drawings to Bordas, but after Bordas declines to make a selection, Artaud sends him notebooks open at the pages at which Artaud has himself chosen drawings to be included; the book's exact number of drawings – eight, finally, following Artaud's earlier proposed figure of twelve – is only fixed at this stage. Artaud is now also complaining about the time that has elapsed since the contract for the book was signed, and demands its immediate publication.

On 16 December 1947, Artaud responds with fury to Bordas's proposal that Artaud should contribute original drawings from his notebooks for a planned special edition (not, in the end, taken forward) of five copies of *Artaud the Mômo*. Artaud complains that everything is being stolen from him, from his opium to his drawings to his writings. But on the following day, having received the finished copies of *Artaud the Mômo*, Artaud wrote again to Bordas, his tone reversed, in his one and only cordial letter of the correspondence: 'Allow me to congratulate you *wholeheartedly*. The edition of my poems *Artaud the Mômo* is a laudable success: page design, typography, the paper used, the format – this is the most beautiful book which has ever appeared in a bookshop. Mr Bordas, you've given me the greatest joy of my career but don't forget the *insistence* with which I demanded that my drawings were to be published on matte paper.'[10]

Artaud's cordial tone in that letter of 16 December 1947 is shattered, and reversed again, in the following, final letter, of 14 February 1948; by that time, *Artaud the Mômo* had finally appeared in Paris's bookshops. In the preceding weeks, Artaud's radio project, *To have done with the judgement of god*, had been censored, refused transmission and attacked in the press. Now, Artaud is furious with Bordas, and as the letter goes on, his handwriting increases in velocity, using gestures of anger rather than punctuation marks, spilling into the margins of the page when it is full: 'Sir, I'm very ill, so ill that when I had a consultation with Prof. Mondor at the Salpêtrière hospital, I was forbidden to leave my bed for several months. So, I can almost never come into Paris. Yesterday, 13 February, I wanted to take advantage of a *very rare* journey into Paris to come and see you.' Bordas's office was located in Montparnasse, in the rue Mouton-Duvernet, not far from the rue Daguerre, where Artaud had stayed in destitution in the studio of the artist René Thomas in the summer of 1937 – often standing in the narrow street outside to demand money from passers-by – immediately before leaving for his apocalyptic journey to Ireland and subsequent asylum incarceration. Bordas's secretary had evidently refused to allow Artaud to enter Bordas's office without an appointment. On that same day's journey into Paris, Artaud also visited heroin dealers in Montmartre, as well as meeting his friend Paule Thévenin, and may have appeared unkempt, desperate, emaciated, and even terrifying, to Bordas's secretary.[11] Now, Artaud is writing at invective speed, beyond punctuation, in his last-words expulsion of fury: '... but my name is Antonin Artaud and you have published one of my books entitled *Artaud the Mômo* which has just sold out in the space of several days... you have made a killing with *Artaud the Mômo* picked up a fortune all that *stinks...*'.[12] Artaud died at his Ivry-sur-Seine pavilion, in the middle of the night of 3-4 March 1948, two weeks later.

This edition of *Artaud the Mômo*, in Clayton Eshleman's translation, was translated from the Gallimard edition of 1974, prepared by Artaud's close collaborator Paule Thévenin, rather than from the Bordas edition of 1948. In preparing her edition (the volume containing *Artaud the Mômo* also includes other poetic texts from Artaud's final period), Thévenin was able to use Artaud's handwritten manuscripts, his drafts of texts inscribed in his notebooks, and the pages of Artaud's dictation which she had transcribed during work on *Artaud the Mômo*. She had kept all of that material in her possession after Artaud's death in 1948. She also incorporated into the Gallimard edition several short post-scriptum additions (not in the Bordas edition) which Artaud had indicated to her that he wanted to be included in the book's poems. This new Diaphanes edition – of Clayton Eshleman's translation into English of *Artaud the Mômo* – is the first since 1948 to present the sequence of five poems as one volume, as Artaud intended.

NOTES

1 Artaud, Notebook 406, 3-4 March 1948, unpublished, collection of the Bibliothèque Nationale de France, Paris.

2 Artaud, Letter of 12 February 1948, unpublished, collection of the Bibliothèque Nationale de France, Paris.

3 Ferlinghetti, Letter of 17 February 1964, unpublished, collection of the Doheny Library, USC, Los Angeles.

4 Thévenin, Letter of 20 November 1965, unpublished, collection of the Doheny Library, USC, Los Angeles.

5 Artaud, Card of 26 December 1946, unpublished, collection of the Bibliothèque Nationale de France, Paris.

6 Artaud, Letter of 6 February 1947, unpublished, collection of the Bibliothèque Nationale de France, Paris.

7 Artaud, Letter of 11 April 1947, unpublished, collection of the Bibliothèque Nationale de France, Paris.

8 Artaud, Letter of 6 May 1947, *L'Arve et l'Aume suivi de 24 lettres à Marc Barbezat*, L'Arbalète, Décines, 1989, page 70.

9 Artaud, Letter of 6 June 1947, unpublished, collection of the Bibliothèque Nationale de France, Paris.

10 Artaud, Letter of 17 December 1947, unpublished, collection of the Bibliothèque Nationale de France, Paris.

11 Information on Artaud's movements on 13 February 1948 given by Paule Thévenin, interview, 2 March 1987.

12 Artaud, Letter of 14 February 1948, unpublished, collection of the Bibliothèque Nationale de France, Paris.

CONTENTS

© DIAPHANES 2020

ISBN 978-3-0358-0235-1

ALL RIGHTS RESERVED

DIAPHANES

HARDSTR. 69 | CH-8004 ZURICH

DRESDENER STR. 118 | D-10999 BERLIN

57 RUE DE LA ROQUETTE | F-75011 PARIS

PRINTED IN GERMANY

LAYOUT: 2EDIT, ZURICH

WWW.DIAPHANES.NET